WEBSTER
and ARNOLD
and the GIANT BOX

WEBSTER
and ARNOLD
and the GIANT BOX

by P.K.Roche

THE DIAL PRESS · NEW YORK

Dial easy-to-read

Published by
The Dial Press
1 Dag Hammarskjold Plaza
New York, New York 10017

Copyright © 1980 by P. K. Roche
All rights reserved. Manufactured in the U.S.A.
First printing

Library of Congress Cataloging in Publication Data
Roche, Patricia K. Webster and Arnold and the giant box.
Summary: Webster and Arnold find a giant box and pretend it
is a cave, a train, a restaurant, a rocket, and a submarine.
[1. Play—Fiction. 2. Boxes—Fiction] I. Title.
PZ7.R585We [E] 80-11595
ISBN 0-8037-9436-3 (lib. bdg.)   ISBN 0-8037-9432-0 (pbk.)

The art for each picture consists of
an ink and wash drawing with two color
overlays, all reproduced as halftone.

CONTENTS

TOO MANY DINOSAURS

One day

Webster and his big brother Arnold

found a giant box.

"Look!" said Webster.

"Someone is throwing this away!"

Arnold gave the box a thump.

"Let's pretend," he said.

"This box can be our cave

and we will be cavemen."

"Great!" said Webster.

Just then Arnold saw something.

"Look," he said.

"Here come some dinosaurs!"

"Hurry," said Webster.

"Let's hide in our cave."

Quickly

they climbed in.

It was dark in the cave.

"We are safe here," said Arnold.

THUMP! THUMP!

The box shook.

"It is the dinosaurs,"

whispered Arnold.

"They want to come in."

THUMP! THUMP! THUMP!

"How can we make them go away?"

asked Webster.

"Let's make a lot of noise

and scare them,"

said Arnold.

"Let's roar!" said Webster.

Webster and Arnold roared.

The thumping stopped.

Then it was very quiet.

Webster and Arnold peeked out
from the cave.

The dinosaurs were running away.

"We sure scared them," said Arnold.

"We sure did," said Webster.

Webster and Arnold came out
of the box.

"We cannot stay here,"
said Arnold.

"There are too many dinosaurs.
Let's take the box home."

BIG BOSS ARNOLD

"No dinosaurs here!" said Webster.

They put the box in the yard.

"Let's pretend

the box is a train now," said Arnold.

"I will be the engineer.

You can be the rider."

16

Arnold pointed.

"Riders sit in back of the box."

"It looks dark there," said Webster.

"Can I ride in the front too?"

"No," said Arnold.

"Only the engineer can ride here.

Ding! Ding!"

"Can I ring the bell?"

asked Webster.

"No," said Arnold.

"Only the engineer rings the bell.

This train is going to Texas.

All aboard!" he called.

Webster walked over to the house.

He sat down on a step

next to Pandy Bear and Old Bunny.

"Hurry up!" called Arnold.

"The train is leaving."

"I am not going to Texas,"

said Webster.

"I am going to Africa.

It is more fun to go there."

"Come on, Webster," said Arnold.

"No," said Webster.

"Why not?" asked Arnold.

"Because you are a BIG BOSS!" yelled Webster.

"You don't let me ride with you. You don't let me ring the bell. You do it all."

Arnold sat down and thought.

"Let's pretend," he said,

"that we are going to Africa."

Webster didn't say anything.

"The train to Africa needs a conductor

to take tickets," said Arnold.

"What else does he do?" said Webster.

"He rides up front with the engineer,"

said Arnold.

Webster didn't move.

"And he rings the bell," said Arnold.

Webster got up.

He picked up Pandy Bear

and Old Bunny.

"Maybe," he said, "we will take this train to Africa."

THE LIONS ARE COMING

"All aboard for Africa!" called Arnold. "Next stop—jungle."

Webster took tickets

from Pandy Bear and Old Bunny.

Then he rode up front with Arnold.

"Look!" said Arnold.

"We are in Africa."

"I see lions," said Webster.

"I think they are following us," said Arnold.

"They are chasing us!"

yelled Webster.

"Hurry! Faster!

The lions are coming!"

"I can't," yelled Arnold.

"We are going at top speed."

"Look!" yelled Webster.

"The lions are all tired out.

We are getting ahead of them!"

"We are safe!" Arnold cried.

Soon a voice called, "Time for lunch."

It was Mother.

"We are in Africa," called Webster.

26

"Are you coming home soon?"
asked Mother.

"We are almost home right now,"
called Arnold.

"No stops," called Webster.

"Ding! Ding!"

"We made it!" said Arnold.

GOING OUT FOR LUNCH

Mother was sitting on a step.

"Welcome home," she said.

"Come in and we will make lunch."

Arnold looked back at the box.

"Mom," he said, "can we pretend the box is a restaurant?"

"Can we eat there?" asked Webster.

"Fine ideas," said Mother.

"I will be the cook," said Webster.

"I will be the waiter," said Arnold.

"And I will be a customer,"
said Mother.

"Hurray!" shouted Webster.
He ran into the kitchen.
He made three peanut butter
and jelly sandwiches.
He poured three cups of milk.
Arnold put everything on a tray.
He carried it to the restaurant.

Then they all ate lunch.

"This is a very fine lunch,"
said Mother.

She looked in her pocket.

She took out two dimes.

She gave one dime to Webster.

"One for the cook," she said.

Webster smiled.

"Thank you," he said.

Mother gave the other dime to Arnold.

"One for the waiter," she said.

"Thank you," said Arnold.

"Come again."

"Oh, I will," said Mother.

"Going out for lunch is fun.

Good-bye now!"

WHAT IS THAT FUNNY NOISE?

It was getting warm.

Webster and Arnold were sitting

next to the box.

"Want to play train again?"

asked Webster.

"No," said Arnold. "That is no fun.

Let's pretend we are on a rocket."

"Oh, boy!" said Webster.

"Who will I be?"

"You will be Rocket Mouse,"

said Arnold.

"And I will be Chief.

Now let's get ready to blast off."

"Okay," said Webster.

"What does Rocket Mouse do?"

"Rocket Mouse helps the Chief,"
said Arnold.

"Sh-h! Here's the countdown."

"But what do I *do*?" yelled Webster.

"Nothing!" yelled Arnold.

"That's what you do!

10...9..."

"Listen," said Webster.

"What is that funny noise?"

"Sh-h!" said Arnold.

"There is no funny noise.

8...7..."

"The rocket is going

wick-ee, wick-ee," said Webster.

"The rocket is not going

wick-ee wick-ee," said Arnold.

"6...5..."

"I think the rocket is going

to explode," said Webster.

"No," said Arnold.

"It is not going to explode.

4...3..."

Webster listened closely.

"Yes," he said.

"I feel sure it is going to explode.
The wick-ee is getting louder."

"It is not!" yelled Arnold.

"The wick-ee is not getting louder!

2 . . . 1 . . . blast—"

"WICK-EE! WICK-EE! KA-POW!"

yelled Webster.

"The rocket is exploding!"

"That does it!" shouted Arnold.

"I'll never play with you again!

Never! Never! Never!"

And he stamped out of the box.

"Good!" Webster called after him.

"I have other things to do—

important things!"

SUBMARINE GOING DOWN

Webster picked up Pandy Bear
and Old Bunny.
"It is too hot here," he said.
They went up a little hill
and sat under a tree.
It was cool there.

Webster closed his eyes.

He could hear the breeze blowing

in the trees.

Whoosh. Whoosh.

It sounds like the ocean, he thought.

Suddenly he opened his eyes

and jumped up.

"Wait here!" he yelled.

"I will be right back."

Webster ran to the box.

He tugged and pulled at it.

The box bumped along slowly.

Finally Webster pushed it

to the top of the hill.

But the box did not stand up anymore.

So Webster leaned it against the tree.

"Let's pretend

the box is our submarine

and I am the Captain," he said.

"We are going to look for treasure."

Webster, Pandy Bear, and Old Bunny
climbed into the box.
Then Webster said in a loud voice,
"Close all hatches, men.
Submarine going down."
Pandy Bear and Old Bunny
were sitting close to each other.
"Don't be afraid," Webster said.

"Look out the window.

Look at all the fish."

They looked out.

Soon they saw sea horses.

They saw a mermaid.

"Now," said Webster,

"we're getting close

to the treasure."

They looked all around

for the treasure.

"Look!" shouted Webster.

"It is in that cave!"

They got closer to the cave.

Webster saw an eye looking out.

Then he saw a long arm...

and another...

and another....

"Octopus!" shouted Webster.

The whole octopus swam out
from the cave.
It swam closer and closer
to the submarine.
The submarine began to shake.
"Help! Octopus!"
cried Webster.

:"No!" yelled a voice from outside.

"It's me! Arnold!"

IT CANNOT BE A FIRE TRUCK

Arnold got into the box.

He was wearing his fireman's hat.

"How come this box is such a mess?"

he asked.

Webster hung his head.

He didn't say a word.

"Well," said Arnold.

"It cannot be a fire truck.

It cannot be anything anymore.

It is falling over."

"Let's pretend, Arnold!"

said Webster.

"It can be a good slide

if we make it fall over all the way."

"That might work," said Arnold.

"But first

we need to jump on it a little."

"Yes!" shouted Webster.

"Let's jump!"

So they jumped on the box—

and jumped—

and jumped

until it was just right.

Flat.

"Let's try it out," said Webster.
So they tried out the slide
and it was fine.